The VERY VISIBLE MOUSE

ANNE MERRICK

Illustrated by

TESSA RICHARDSON-JONES

For
Harry, Holly, Gene and Sally with love
TRJ

Tom, Hannah, Becca and Josh
AM

First published in Great Britain in 1995
This paperback edition published 1997

Text © 1995 Anne Merrick
Illustration © 1995 Tessa Richardson-Jones

The moral right of the author has been asserted

Bloomsbury Publishing PLC, 38 Soho Square, London W1V 5DF

A CIP catalogue record for this book is available from The British Library

ISBN 0 7475 3063 7

THE
VERY
VISIBLE
MOUSE

ANNE MERRICK

Illustrated by

TESSA RICHARDSON-JONES

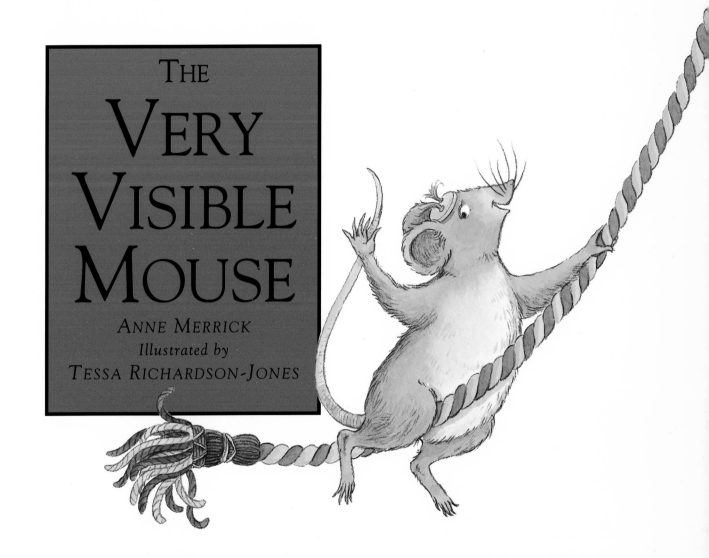

Bloomsbury Children's Books

Once upon a time there was a house. The house belonged to Mr and Mrs Jones but they shared it with the Dog – who lived in a basket – the parrot – who lived in a cage – and a Tribe of Mice who lived in every nook and cranny, every crack and crevice and every hole and corner.

The head of the Tribe of Mice was Serendipity – Great-Great-Grandfather Serendipity. He was the oldest and largest and wisest of the mice. Then there was Serenity and Solemnity, Homity, Dimity and Alacrity, One-Eyed Oddity and Dignity and dozens and dozens of lesser Mousitys right down to the loveliest and liveliest - but silliest Mouse whose name was CALAMITY.

Serendipity was fond of lecturing his family, especially on Sundays.

"This house is OUR WORLD," he said. "And if you want to survive in this world, you will keep a VERY LOW PROFILE."

"Oh dear! Oh deary!" fussed Homity.

"What does he mean?" asked Calamity. "I don't know what he means!"

"He means stay out of sight, man!" drawled Serenity, preening his whiskers. "Don't get VISIBLE!"

Pepper Spray

Catapult

Flying machine

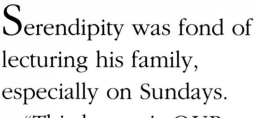

"Moreover," continued Serendipity, "it is the policy of this mousehold that every mouse should, as far as possible, avoid all DANGEROUS SITUATION situations."

"Now what does he mean?" asked Calamity, who was growing bored and beginning to frolic about.

"He meanth," snapped Dimity, "you muthn't have fun!"

"Hm. Hah. Indeed!" agreed Dignity.

All that Mr and Mrs Jones ever saw of Serendipity and his family, was the flick of Alacrity's tail when she scuttled under the skirting, or the flash of Oddity's eye as he whisked beneath the wardrobe. And because the house was always dimpsy and their sight was rather dim, they had no idea they'd seen a mouse at all. The Dog didn't believe in Mice. It was only the Parrot, busy practising words, who noticed anything.

"WATCH OUT," she squawked. "IN THE JEWEL BOX! OH CALAMITY!"

Poor Calamity! She crept away to a comfortable place she knew on the sofa and she thought, "I am what I am. I am no good at all at keeping a LOW PROFILE and I am hopeless at avoiding DANGEROUS SITUATION situations. I am a VERY VISIBLE MOUSE who likes a bit of fun. Surely," she said to herself, "there must be a place in the world for a mouse like me!"

SO . . .

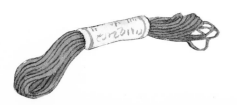

. . . When Mr and Mrs Jones hobbled in to clear the supper, Calamity was frolicking on the floor. She frisked and whisked and gambolled and tumbled.

"Bless my heart!" said Mrs Jones. "There's a MOUSE about our house. We shall have to set a trap!"

Then Calamity sang. She warbled and fluted and yodelled and tooted.

"Did you ever!" said Mr Jones. "This house has got a MOUSE. We shall have to get a cat!"

"But a mouse has got to do," said Calamity, "what a mouse has got to do." So Calamity danced. She pranced and pirouetted. She tangoed and fandangoed. She skipped and hopped and jived and bopped. She had never danced so hard in all her life.

"Help!" squeaked the mice in their hiding places.

"Olé!" cried Mrs Jones.

"Bravo!" cried Mr Jones

"Wow!" howled the Dog. "Wow-ow-ow-ow!"

And the Parrot, lost for words, hung upside down from her perch and SCREECHED.

"**W**hat a MOUSE to have about the house," said Mr and Mrs Jones."We CAN'T set a trap! We'll NEVER get a cat!'

Then Serendipity and Serenity and Solemnity, Homity, Dimity and Alacrity, One-eyed Oddity and Dignity and all the Tribe of lesser Mousitys, whistled and jiggled and cheered and clapped.

"My dear Family," said Serendipity. "It seems to me that we are SAVED! Let's have a PARTY!"

So every night from then on, Calamity enjoyed being a VERY VISIBLE MOUSE. And she had a lot of fun.

People came from far and near to see and cheer her. On the night of her hundredth performance, she said to her Tribe, "I have found my place in the world. What's more, I have saved us all from a most DANGEROUS SITUATION situation. And though I am what I am, I am not a CALAMITY. What I AM," she said, as they tied her bows and powdered her nose, "is a . . .

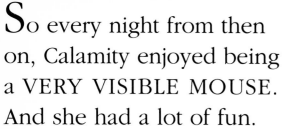

CELEBRITY!"